Barbie
of
Swan Lake

A Junior Novelization

Adapted by Linda Aber

Based on the screenplay by
Cliff Ruby & Elana Lesser

SCHOLASTIC INC.

New York   Toronto   London   Auckland   Sydney
Mexico City   New Delhi   Hong Kong   Buenos Aires

Introduction

Once upon a time, in a faraway land where unicorns lived and sorcerers cast magic spells, there was a young girl named Odette. She was a beautiful, sweet girl, but very shy. Odette stayed at home and helped her father in the family bakery. Her sister, Marie, was the brave one, always having adventures. But little did Odette know that she was about to have an adventure of her own in a lovely and mysterious place called Swan Lake. . . .

P9-DJL-838

Chapter 1
The Unicorn

"Marie! Be careful!" Odette gasped. Her sister's horse galloped at top speed and jumped over a fence. "Any faster and you'll be flying!"

"That's the idea!" Marie laughed. She rode up to the bakery window, where Odette was busy working with their father. "Come on, Odette," she said. "I'm heading out again. You'll love it!"

Odette came out to meet her sister. Suddenly, the horse reared up. Odette jumped back in fear.

"I'll be back to help soon," Marie said with a wave.

Odette's father poked his head out of the shop. "Was that your sister?" he asked.

"Here and gone, Papa." Odette sighed. "Flying like the wind."

Odette and Marie were so different. Marie was the daring one, while Odette was shy and timid. But that was okay — she loved helping her father in the bakery. Odette turned back to her baking and hummed a pretty tune while she moved around the kitchen.

As she wiped flour off her dress, Odette heard shouts from down the street. "Look at that! Do you see it? There it goes! Hurry!"

Odette looked out the window. She couldn't believe her eyes. Dashing through the streets was a real unicorn! Right behind it was a group of villagers. They were trying to capture it!

"Don't let it get away!" they shouted.

Odette ran after the crowd. She found them just in time to see one of the villagers

aiming his bow and arrow at the beautiful creature. "Wait! You'll hurt her!" Odette cried.

But it was too late. Odette gasped as she watched the creature dodge the arrow.

The unicorn glanced back at the wild crowd. The people were running at her with ropes, bows and arrows, and burlap sacks.

She had to get away! The unicorn dashed toward a cart loaded with firewood. Using her horn, she moved a rock that blocked the cart's wheel. The cart rolled backward — straight for the villagers!

"Watch out!" someone shouted as the runaway cart raced toward the group. Firewood flew through the air, just missing people's heads.

Just when the unicorn seemed safe, a lasso landed around her neck and pulled her to the ground.

"Got it!" shouted a burly man. He was holding the other end of the rope. "A real unicorn! This should fetch a pretty price!"

"No!" Odette cried. But before she could think of a way to free the unicorn, the animal escaped on her own! She pulled the rope across the blade of a nearby ax and cut it! The villager at the other end of the rope flew backward and landed in a barrel.

While the other villagers laughed at the man, the unicorn disappeared. Only Odette saw the beautiful animal heading for the forest outside the village. And only Odette saw the long rope that was dangling

from the unicorn's neck get tangled in a bush.

"Oh, no!" Odette cried. "Trapped again!" She raced toward the unicorn, determined to help her. Odette followed the unicorn through the thick trees of the forest.

Suddenly, Odette felt something grab her. She turned to see what horrible thing was holding her, but the monster she feared was just a branch catching on her dress.

Almost at the same time, the unicorn tugged free from the bush that held her. She led the way to a beautiful waterfall, crossing the stream on a fallen tree.

Odette followed close behind. As she stepped onto the tree bridge, Odette looked down at the rushing water and became afraid. "Oh!" she cried. "I can't go any farther."

At that moment the unicorn's legs got tangled in the dangling rope. The creature tripped and her back legs slipped off the bridge. She was going to fall!

"Hold on!" Odette cried, running across the bridge toward the struggling unicorn.

When the unicorn looked up and saw a human coming, she scrambled to her feet and ran toward the foaming water of the waterfall.

In spite of her fears, Odette inched her way across the stream and toward the waterfall. Right before her eyes, the unicorn's horn began to glow magically. The unicorn touched its tip to a huge boulder. The boulder began to sparkle. Then it slid open, revealing a secret passageway. The unicorn slipped through the opening. Odette was right behind her as the boulder slid back into place, sealing them both inside!

Chapter 2
The Magic Crystal

Odette made her way through the secret tunnel, barely able to see except for the light on the other side. By the time she reached the end, the unicorn was out of sight. Odette had entered a new forest, one that was different from the one on the other side of the waterfall.

Odette looked around curiously until a frightened cry from the unicorn caught her attention. She followed the sound until she came to the most breathtaking place she'd ever seen. It was Swan Lake, shimmering in light. It was surrounded by flowers and weeping willows.

Near the banks of the lake, the unicorn was struggling in a patch of brambles. The rope was twisted around her neck. Odette ran to help her. "Hold still," she said. She tried to untangle the rope.

"Easy for you to say," the unicorn said. "You're not getting strangled!"

"You talk?" Odette exclaimed.

"Of course," the unicorn replied. "Now, are you going to stand around with your mouth open, or cut me loose?"

Odette smiled. "I guess you haven't heard of the word 'please,'" she said.

"You sound just like the Fairy Queen,"

the unicorn replied. "Never mind. I'll do it myself." The unicorn tugged, but the rope only cut deeper. "Ouch!" she gasped.

"Hang on," Odette cried. "I'll cut it with something."

Odette pushed through the brush. She was looking for something sharp. Soon she discovered a beautiful crystal with sharp edges stuck in a tree. It was exactly what Odette needed to cut the rope.

Odette pulled the crystal free and rushed back to the unicorn to cut the rope. "There," she said. "I thought that would do the trick."

At that moment, the Fairy Queen of the forest and her followers stepped out from the trees. Odette's eyes opened wide

in surprise. Who were these beautiful creatures?

"Did you see that, Your Highness?" the unicorn asked. "She used the crystal."

"I'm terribly s-sorry," Odette stammered.

"Please don't apologize," the Fairy Queen said kindly. "We've been waiting for you for a long time. The Magic Crystal belongs to you now."

"Me?" said Odette. "You must have me mixed up with somebody else."

"The crystal belongs to her?" Lila the unicorn asked. "How is *she* going to save *us*?"

"Let me explain to both of you," the Fairy Queen answered.

Chapter 3
The Evil Rothbart

Odette sat wide-eyed as she listened to the Fairy Queen explain how the Enchanted Forest had become a dangerous place for everyone in it.

"Years ago, my cousin Rothbart lived in the Enchanted Forest with us," the queen began. "He had an evil plan to rule the forest. When it came time for our uncle, the king, to choose the next ruler, he chose me instead of Rothbart. Rothbart was very, very angry. So he left."

"Forever?" Odette asked.

The Fairy Queen sighed. "No, not forever. For many years all was well. Then Rothbart came back with his daughter, Odile. He used his dark magic to turn some of my bravest fairies and elves into animals. And he began taking over the forest."

Lila stepped forward. "But now you're here," she said to Odette. "Rothbart's gonna meet his match!"

"I don't understand," said Odette.

"It's been foretold that the one who frees the Magic Crystal will save our home," the Fairy Queen explained. "But nobody has ever been able to pull the crystal from the tree until today."

Two of the Fairy Queen's court, Ivan and

Carlita, danced around Odette. "Our hero!" they sang.

"Please," Odette said, "you have the wrong girl. I wish I could help, but I've got to get back to my family. I'm sorry."

"I understand, Odette," said the Fairy Queen. "Lila will show you the way out."

"Good-bye," said Odette sadly. "I'm sorry."

Lila led the way toward the passage. "If I had that Magic Crystal," she said, "I'd get rid of Rothbart once and for all."

"It's just — I'm not brave like you," Odette replied.

At that moment, a large shadow fell across the path. Odette and Lila looked up to see two dark creatures swooping down.

To Odette's shock, one transformed into a towering, evil-looking man with piercing eyes. The other turned into a mean-looking girl dripping with jewels.

"It's Rothbart and Odile!" Lila exclaimed.

Rothbart laughed evilly. "A little bird whispered in my ear that some human girl freed the Magic Crystal. It couldn't be you, could it?" he growled at Odette.

"That's right!" Lila snapped at Rothbart. "Odette's gonna have you for breakfast, 'cause you two are toast!"

Rothbart smiled a nasty smile as he raised his fist. The magic ring on his finger flashed a ray of light at Odette. The ray became a whirling comet and surrounded her in a spinning cloud of evil magic.

Lila watched helplessly as the cloud dissolved. Odette was gone — and in her place was a beautiful swan!

Rothbart laughed. "Now look at the great hero of the forest!"

Odette lifted her wings and tried to fly. But she wasn't used to them, and they just

flapped at her sides. Just as she was about to give up, the Fairy Queen and her court arrived.

"We came as quickly as we could," the queen said, placing a beautiful crown on Odette's head. The Magic Crystal glowed in the center of the silver band. "This will protect you," the queen said. "Rothbart can do nothing more to you as long as you wear the crystal."

"That's what you think, cousin!" Rothbart hissed. "Soon even your powers won't protect you. This is my forest. Why don't you save us all a lot of trouble and hand over the crown?"

"Never," the Fairy Queen declared.

Rothbart flashed his magical ring at

Odette. "Then she's coming with me!" he roared.

As the flash of the ring shot toward the Magic Crystal, Odette's crown glowed with magic of its own. It was protecting her, just as the queen had said it would!

Rothbart was angry. "Is this your idea of a game?" he demanded.

"Leave this place, Rothbart," the Fairy Queen ordered. "You can do nothing here."

Rothbart and Odile transformed back into their birdlike forms and flew away. But the Fairy Queen knew her cousin would be back soon enough, with another plan more evil than the first one.

Chapter 4
The Troll and the
Book of Forest Lore

"You got him!" Lila cheered.

Odette looked sadly at her swan wings. "I think he got me," she said with a sigh. She turned to the Fairy Queen. "Can you turn me back?"

The queen looked at her half-glowing wand and shook her head. "My powers aren't strong enough to break his spell completely," she admitted. "The most I could do for the elves and fairies when he turned them into animals was to turn them back to themselves from sunset until dawn. But my powers are not as strong now as they were then."

Odette noticed that the sun was sinking behind the trees. Soon it would be night. "Please try," she cried. "Please. I don't want to be a swan for the rest of my life."

The Fairy Queen aimed her wand at Odette. The wand flickered, but only a weak burst of magic came out.

"It'll work," Lila said hopefully. "It's got to."

Odette watched as, one by one, the other animals magically transformed back into their elf selves. Only Odette remained trapped in the form of a swan.

The queen tried one more time. Suddenly, in a shower of magical sprinkles, Odette transformed back into her human form. Everyone cheered. But the Fairy Queen reminded Odette, "Once the sun rises, you will be a swan again."

"There must be some secret to stopping Rothbart," Odette said hopefully.

"There is a secret in the *Book of Forest Lore*," the queen said. "But that book can only be opened by the one who has the crystal." The queen plucked a large leaf off a tree and touched it with her wand. "The book is guarded by a troll named Erasmus. Take this leaf with my mark on it. It will unlock the door to the vault where the book is stored."

With Lila leading the way, Odette set out
on her most dangerous journey yet. Lila's
glowing horn showed the way along the
banks of the moonlit lake. Soon she and
Odette reached a brightly colored toadstool. "Here we are," Lila said.

Odette pulled out the leaf with the Fairy

Queen's mark on it. Instantly, the mark of the queen sparkled, and the doors on the toadstool opened.

A dark stairway led to a large wooden door. Lila stepped forward, then looked back. "Come on," she said to Odette. "Hey, you're braver than you think!"

"At least one of us thinks so," Odette said as she started down the stairway.

"Who goes there?" a gruff voice boomed.

"It's m-me, Lila, and my friend Odette," Lila stammered. "The Fairy Queen sent us to see the *Book of Forest Lore*."

The door slowly creaked open. By the light of Lila's glowing horn, they saw a troll with wild hair, pointy nails, and dark eyes. He looked terrifying! But when he learned who they were and why they had come, Erasmus was happy to help.

Together, Lila, Odette, and the troll spent the whole night looking through the crowded bookshelves. Finally, at dawn, Erasmus dropped his stack of books. "That does it. I give up," he said.

The sun was rising. Odette glimpsed

herself in a mirror, and tears sprang to her eyes. It was morning, and she had turned into a swan again. But she held her head up, determined to find the answer. "Which shelf next, Erasmus?"

Chapter 5
The Prince

Late that afternoon, Odette returned to Swan Lake. She had spent the day with Erasmus, but they had not found the *Book of Forest Lore*. She was a swan again, and she was very tired. So she floated on the lake for a nap.

While Odette slept, the shadow of Rothbart swooped down on her. Odette awoke just in time to fly away.

Rothbart chased Odette toward the other bank. The evil sorcerer had a new plan. He could not harm Odette while she wore the Magic Crystal, but a human could. So Rothbart had lured the kingdom's young prince, Daniel, to the side of the lake. A beautiful swan would be quite a prize for the prince on his hunt!

Odette was flying so furiously to get away from Rothbart, she didn't see the handsome young man taking aim with his bow and arrow. He had a clear shot as he pulled back on the bow.

"Now!" Rothbart muttered under his breath. "Shoot her!"

Prince Daniel was ready to release the arrow when the lovely bird arched against the last rays of the sun. The prince paused. "So beautiful!" he said, lowering his bow.

He couldn't bear to shoot such a wonderful creature.

Odette landed near the lake. She didn't notice the prince as he moved closer and watched in awe as she transformed back into her human self.

"Who are you?" Prince Daniel breathed.

Odette looked up with surprise. She recognized the prince right away. "My name is Odette, Your Highness," she said.

"You know me?" said the prince.

"I live in the village," Odette replied. "At least I did until . . ."

"Until what?" Daniel asked.

Odette told him her unbelievable story. The prince listened intently.

"And so now," Odette finished, "I

have to break Rothbart's spell. Somehow . . ."

At that moment, Rothbart swooped down from the sky and slashed at the prince with sharp claws. The prince jumped back in alarm as Rothbart transformed into his human form.

"One arrow from a human!" Rothbart sneered. "That's all it would have taken to kill her! You're as useless as a pig!" He raised his ring to turn the prince into a pig.

"Stop!" Odette cried. She threw herself in front of the prince to block Rothbart's blast.

"Give me your crown and I'll leave him alone," Rothbart growled.

The prince fired an arrow at Rothbart,

but the sorcerer flashed his magic ring and created a force field around himself. The arrow bounced away harmlessly.

Rothbart fired another blast at the prince, but once again Odette stepped in the way. The power of the Magic Crystal protected them both, and again Rothbart left empty-handed.

The prince was amazed. "Thank you," he said. "You saved me."

"I'm glad you're all right," Odette replied.

Odette and the prince walked hand in hand around the lake, taking in the marvelous sights. There were magical creatures everywhere — dancing flowers,

twirling fairies, mischievous pixies. The prince began to fall under the forest's spell — and under Odette's. "I'll never forget this," the prince said.

"I'm glad, Your Highness," Odette replied, gazing into his eyes.

"Tomorrow night," the prince said, "my mother is throwing a royal ball. Will you

come with me as my honored guest?"

Odette was thrilled. But even her happiness couldn't stop the sun from rising. "It's almost dawn!" she whispered.

The prince took Odette's hand. "Come with me," he said. "I can protect you at my castle. You can bring your family. Please."

Odette wanted to be with the prince.

And she wanted to see her family and be safe. But then she thought of Lila and her other new friends. "I can't," she said, touching the crystal. "I need to stay here and help the creatures of the forest. But please, find my family and tell them I'm all right. I'll break the spell somehow."

"I'm staying with you," the prince said.

"No, go home," Odette said softly. "I'll come tomorrow night. I promise." Then, right before his eyes, she transformed into a swan again.

The prince watched sadly as Odette glided off into the lake. He had no choice but to leave her behind.

Chapter 6
Rothbart's Evil Plan

"I found it!" Erasmus shouted, waving the *Book of Forest Lore* in the air. Then he ran to Swan Lake as fast as his troll legs would take him. He found Odette and the others in their human and elf forms.

"Well done, Erasmus," the Fairy Queen said, taking the book from the troll. She passed it to Odette.

The crystal in Odette's crown glowed as the book magically flew open. Odette began reading aloud. *"'The one who frees the Magic*

Crystal will share a love so true, so pure, it will overcome all evil magic.'"

"You and the prince!" Lila exclaimed.

"Wait, Lila," Odette said, and she continued reading. *"'If, however, the true love pledges love to another, the Magic Crystal will lose its power.'"*

"The legend cannot be changed," the Fairy Queen said. "We must get you ready for the ball tonight. You must dance in the arms of the prince. And as you dance, he will declare his true love for you."

Just then, out of nowhere, Rothbart swooped down and grabbed Erasmus and the *Book of Forest Lore*. He carried them away in his sharp claws.

"Help!" Erasmus cried.

"Oh, no!" the Fairy Queen cried. "Erasmus will be all right. It's the book that Rothbart wants."

The Fairy Queen was right. Rothbart read the book and learned that the Magic Crystal's powers could be broken. He came up with a plan. "Odile," he said to his daughter, "tonight, at the royal ball, you

must dance with the prince."

Rothbart touched his magic ring to the ruby pendant around Odile's neck. The jewel began to glow. "It's magic now," he said. "Every time the prince looks at you, he'll see his 'true love,' that silly Odette girl."

"So?" Odile said.

"The prince will declare his love to you," Rothbart explained. "The powers of the Magic Crystal will be lost, and I will take over as ruler of the Enchanted Forest!"

✻　✻　✻

That evening, Prince Daniel was dressed in his finest clothes and looking more handsome than ever. He waited and

watched for Odette. He hoped she would keep her promise to come to the ball.

At that very moment, Rothbart and Odile entered the ballroom. Rothbart flashed his magic ring at his own face and made himself look like Odette's father. On his arm was Odile.

When Prince Daniel caught sight of

Odile, the magic of her jeweled pendant worked. To Daniel, Odile appeared to be Odette!

"I'm so glad you came!" Prince Daniel said. "Will you dance with me?"

Thinking he had Odette in his arms, the prince whispered to his dance partner, "I promised my mother I'd find myself a bride tonight," he said. "And I never break a promise!"

Rothbart stood in the shadows, delighted his plan was working so well. But then he was distracted by a sound above him. Looking up, he saw Odette as a swan flying toward the ballroom doors!

Rothbart quickly fired a blast from his ring. The doors slammed shut just as

46

Odette was about to fly through them!

But Odette was determined to get in. She flew to a window and looked into the ballroom — only to see the prince and Odile dancing! "No!" cried Odette. But once again Rothbart used his magic to shut her out.

Meanwhile, Daniel and Odile continued to dance. The prince looked deeply into Odile's eyes. "I guess what I'm asking is," he said, "will you marry me?"

"I couldn't help overhearing, Your Highness," Rothbart said, stepping up to the couple. "You are asking for my daughter's hand in marriage. But do you love her?"

The prince gazed at Odile with eyes

blinded by magic. "Yes," he said. "I love her with all my heart."

Suddenly, thunder boomed and a bolt of lightning flashed in the ballroom. Outside the window, Odette was gasping for breath. The glow of the Magic Crystal was fading away. Without its magic to save her, Odette fell to the ground, senseless!

Back inside the ballroom, Rothbart was gloating. "Thank you, Your Highness," he said. "You've been very helpful."

To the prince's horror, Odile pulled off the magic pendant and returned to her usual human form. Prince Daniel realized he'd been tricked!

"Where's Odette?" he cried.

"Too late," Rothbart sneered. "You've already pledged your love to Odile."

The prince and all the guests backed away in horror as Rothbart and Odile transformed into their birdlike selves and flew out of the ballroom.

Chapter 7
The Final Battle

The sun cast its last pink rays over Odette as she lay unconscious, still in the form of a swan. As the sun sank from view, she transformed back into her beautiful human form. With her blond hair around her face and her lovely ball gown spread around her, Odette looked like a princess. But the Magic Crystal in her crown no longer glowed or sparkled. The magic was gone.

"Let's see how brave you are without the

crystal!" Rothbart snickered, standing over her. He plucked the crystal from the crown and put it on a chain around his neck.

Rothbart was enjoying his victory. "You didn't really think you could beat me, did you?" he cackled to the sleeping girl. "Here's a prediction: You're never going to wake up!" He aimed his magic ring at Odette.

Before Rothbart could fire the magic from the ring, Prince Daniel jumped down from the castle wall, his sword flashing! He charged at Rothbart, but Rothbart's magic turned the sword into a harmless feather!

Thinking fast, the prince grabbed a pole and used it like a spear. Looking past Rothbart, Prince Daniel saw Lila and the Fairy

Queen coming to help save Odette. Lila was pulling the Fairy Queen's carriage. He knew if he could keep Rothbart busy, Lila and the Fairy Queen could carry Odette to safety.

With Rothbart flashing more magic at him, the prince ducked behind Odile just in time. The blast hit her and turned her into a pig!

While the prince battled with Rothbart, Lila and the Fairy Queen lifted Odette into the carriage. "Go!" cried the Fairy Queen.

"The girl is getting away!" Rothbart shouted as he watched the queen's carriage disappear into the woods. Quickly he changed into his birdlike form and flew after the carriage.

The carriage wound through the trees and finally reached the waterfall. A team of the queen's fairies carried the carriage as Lila ran across the bridge. But before they could escape, Rothbart blocked their path.

"Leave the girl," the Fairy Queen demanded. "Your battle is with me."

"You're right, cousin," Rothbart

shouted. He flashed his magic ring at the queen and transformed her into a white mouse! And he wasn't finished yet. "Now for the girl!" he snarled, moving toward the carriage where Odette lay unconscious.

Meanwhile, Prince Daniel was racing into the forest on horseback. He arrived in time to shoot an arrow at Rothbart. But

Rothbart whirled around and fired a magical twister at the arrow, and the arrow turned into a shower of sparkles.

Odette, stirring in the back of the carriage, was slowly awakening. She sat up and looked around just in time to see Rothbart backing Prince Daniel against a tree.

"Did you really think you could stop me?" Rothbart snarled at the prince.

"No!" Odette cried. "Don't hurt him!" She ran to save the prince.

"Odette," Prince Daniel shouted, "you don't have the crystal to protect you!"

Rothbart aimed his magic ring at the prince. Odette leaped in front of the prince to block the evil magic of the ring. Almost as quickly, the prince put himself in front of Odette. In one terrible strike, both Odette and the prince were hit by Rothbart's dark magic. With their hands clasped together, the prince and Odette sank to the ground, lifeless.

Rothbart laughed evilly. "Not a bad deal," he snickered. "Two for one! At last this world is mine!"

Rothbart didn't see the Magic Crystal around his neck beginning to glow brighter and brighter.

But Lila did. "The legend!" she cried. "It must be true love . . . the crystal's power isn't gone!"

Suddenly powerless, Rothbart tried to pull the Magic Crystal off. Sparks flew from it. Rothbart gasped in shock. In seconds the power of the crystal lifted Rothbart off the ground. A magical glow surrounded him, turning him into a glowing ball. Thunder clapped. Sparks of lightning shot out from the ball. With a final burst of energy, the ball broke into a million pieces. Only a few feathers and the Magic Crystal were left. Rothbart was gone for good.

At the same moment, Odette and Prince Daniel stirred. Slowly, they sat up.

"Odette?" the prince said.

"Are you all right?" Odette asked him.

"Rothbart tricked me. It's you I love," the prince declared. "Will you marry me?"

"Oh, yes!" Odette said happily. The prince took her in his arms.

"We owe you everything, Odette," the Fairy Queen said.

Odette smiled as she spoke to the crowd of friends standing on the bank of Swan Lake. "A wise unicorn once told me you're braver than you think," she said. "It turns out she was right."

Lila's horn glowed as she looked at Odette with pride and gratitude. Swan Lake was always a magical place, but thanks to Odette, now it would be a happy place as well.

A few days later, Odette and the prince were married, with all their friends and family around them. And they lived happily ever after.